All Santa's Reindeer

Written by Lorry Brackett and Illustrated by Joe Brackett

Thank You

Joe, my love, for all the beautiful illustrations. Your unique and playful style has made these stories come to life. And for your encouragement during this project, and providing this opportunity for us.

Abe, my wordsmith son, for brilliant 'child-it-down' editing. Your combination of writing and having six kids is exactly what I needed.

Jess, my very caring daughter. Your awareness, sensitivity, and caring about how things are portrayed, kept my thoughts on track.

Ramona, my dear friend. Your editing skills for English, grammar, punctuation and flow were invaluable.

Halgas, my sweet neighbor. Your suggestions and patience in reading and rereading changed my format for the better.

Denise and Cindy, two of my sisters. Thanks for your interest in reading, correcting, and giving me honest feedback and opinions. So valuable.

Cheryl Collins, Christa Berthold, and Mary LaBianca for being such enthusiastic readers, and for sharing their knowledge and insight.

A special thanks to my granddaughter Faith, whose keen eyes and taste for reading, still caught errors after all the other editors.

These books are dedicated to the

Wonder, Resilience, and Adventure

of childhood

Dr. Tao

Sir Wilbur

Baby Dasher

Elder Dasher

Seeker Reindeer

Table of Contents

<u>DASHER</u>

1. The Newest Fawn

The first ray of sunshine was coming over the snow- covered hill. All the reindeer slowly started to awaken from a long night's sleep. Hundreds of hoofs and legs of all sizes started to move. Then, all the tails joined in!

There were white tails, brown tails, big tails, and little tails. As the herd of reindeer felt more warmth from the sun, all their tails wiggled briskly. This was a happy start for a new day.

"I like living at the North Pole," said a little Prancer Reindeer. "I love my thick furry coat that keeps me warm." All the Baby Reindeer stay close to their moms and dads too, because they like staying warm.

This morning is the very first morning for new baby Dasher. He was born last night, on one of the coldest nights ever. His Mom, Bonnie Dasher, felt like he was about to be born, so she hurried back to the barn. A few reindeer saw her hurrying, and guided her into her soft, straw-filled stable, where her new baby was born safe and warm.

"A new fawn to join the herd!" a reindeer cheered. Soon all the reindeer came to view this new little treasure.

"What long legs like his Grandfather," said Elder Comet. Everyone remembered the fawn's Grandfather, Clayton Dasher. He was one of the best Dasher runners ever! His fast running helped him have the best 'take-offs' for Santa's heavy sleigh.

Mrs. Claus, looking at the barn outside her kitchen window, saw all the commotion. There were animals, elves and birds, all in and out of the barn in a flurry.

"What's going ON out there?" she thought. She put on her shawl and earmuffs and hurried out to the barn. There, she saw a new baby reindeer struggling to stand up!

"Oh my, our new Baby Dasher is here!" she said. Everyone watched as Mrs. Claus knelt down and hugged the newborn. Jessica Claus had a very gentle way with animals. Baby Dasher sniffed her shawl that held all the yummy smells of her kitchen.

"Look at you," she said, "You're just a baby, and you're trying to stand up already! My, my! Well, let's give it a try, then. Up you go now, nice and steady."

With her cheerful smile and her steady hands guiding him, baby Dasher stood for all to see. The barn full of friends cheered.

His family named him Donny Dasher, and as he grew and grew, boy did he love playing! Donny had lots of friends, to play with all day.

He said to his best friend Blitzy, "Let's run for as long as we can!"
Swoosh! They would come sliding in on their hind legs! Donny was
laughing, but he always came in second. Blitzy would always beat him back

to the barn. That was OK, because they were best friends. Still, Donny wished he could get there first...just once.

Blitzy said, "Don't worry Donny, when it's time for school, you'll be faster than anyone. You're a Dasher, remember?"

2. Reindeer School

In time, Donny Dasher and Blitzy were old enough to start Reindeer School. There's so much to learn in Reindeer School! Being in charge of Santa's deliveries **AND** Santa's safety is so important. There's flight school, delivering presents, knowing where to go, and of course, weather. Donny Dasher knew that his 'power-slide and 'edge-stop' were excellent. He still needed lots of practice with his 'high-jump' and 'take-offs', but he wasn't really worried.

Every morning at breakfast, he still couldn't eat the sour berries that his Mom gathered. Donny never liked those yucky berries, so he always just kinda' buried them.

"Thanks Mom. I love these pine cones and nuts," Donny said.

His mom replied, "Make sure you eat the berries, too. Young Dashers need them."

Donny secretly slid the awful berries sideways. He covered them with snow and dirt, just like he always did. He never liked that sour taste.

Then a fawn called out, "Come on, Donny, it's our first day of school...let's hurry!"

They cheerfully galloped off to the Skills Meadow for their lessons

"I love it here! Look at all the fawns...everyone's so excited!" said Donny to his new friends at school.

Donny said to his friend, "Blitzy, you time me for the long-prance, and then I'll time you."

They ran all around the edge of the corral, played some 'chase and slide' games, and learned how to take turns. Donny and Blitzy were EXTRA smart in weather class, too. They also learned how important it is to take care of their budding antlers.

Antlers are very important weather tools for flying Santa's sleigh.

The next day in flight class Donny was trying to do 'take-offs'.

"Wow!" he cried, "That was really hard. I didn't get off the ground even once."

Blitzy said, "I saw you trying, Donny. What's stopping you?"

"I don't know, Blitzy. I'll try

harder tomorrow," Donny answered sadly.

The next day Donny whined to his friend, "Oh, my legs are so stiff. I've tried and tried, and they just won't bend enough for 'take-offs'. I have to get off the ground...Dashers are the major lifters of the sleigh!"

Blitzy answered, "Don't worry Donny, we'll get you in the air. Let's go to Spruce Wood tomorrow and practice together. We'll try something new!"

Donny thought that was a good idea, because other fawns were doing their 'take-offs' already. The next day they tried a walking start, a running start, and a leaping start. None of this worked. But, Blitzy had saved his best idea for last.

"Let's get you really high up in a tree, then you'll already be in the air," Blitzy said.

"But I'm scared Blitzy...I've never been in the air," whined Donny.

"You're a Dasher Donny, you have to try," begged Blitzy.

"OK, I guess it's my last chance. Help me get up this tree Blitzy," Donny said. Donny stood up on a really high, big branch.

"This is scary Blitzy, I'm up so high! OK, here goes," he whined.
He was in the air for only about a second. Then he fell down onto the second
big branch... right on his belly!

"Ouch, that was really dumb!" he said when he finally caught his
breath.

"I don't know what else to do," said Blitzy. "Here, slide down onto my back, and I'll take you home."

"OOOHHH……..OK," cried Donny.

Other fawns at school noticed his struggle with 'take- offs', too. One evening Donny heard a fawn say, "Did you see him trying to get off the ground again?" Another fawn said, "He should just give it up." "Maybe he'll never fly" and "Why doesn't he just stick to weather school?" were some of the other comments.

Donny thought to himself, "I just HAVE to fly, no matter what, I just HAVE to!"

3. Sir Wilbur and Dr. Tao

After a while of trying, and hearing all the whispers, Donny was tired. He asked Blitzy, "I don't know what to do anymore. Everyone knows that Dashers are supposed to be the best flyers. Maybe I should talk to the teacher."

Blitzy grinned and his eyes opened wide, "Yeah, maybe Sir Wilbur can help! He's a great teacher."

Donny replied, "But he's so busy with all the flight classes."

Blitzy pleaded, "You've gotta try, Donny. You're a Dasher, remember?"

Donny knew it was his only chance to fly. The next day after school, he waited on the practice runway at the Skills Meadow so he could talk to his teacher.

Sir Wilbur, the flight teacher, had grand antlers and he was very wise. He said, "My, how hard you work at 'take-offs,' my son. It's rare to see such dedication."

"Thank you, Sir," said Donny, "but I'm so tired and all this practice isn't working. I just wanna get off the ground, and be a real Dasher."

Sir Wilbur suggested, "Well, let's look at WHY 'take-offs' are so hard for you."

"OK," said Donny, still discouraged. "I'm starting to think that I'm just not good enough."

Sir Wilbur assured Donny, "You are indeed good enough and we'll solve this puzzle. Get a good night's rest and meet me here in the morning." Donny was so tired that he just yawned and strolled back to his family stall.

While Donny lay sleeping, Sir Wilbur found his friend Dr. Tao. She's the doctor for all the animals of the North Pole. He knew she would gladly help.

Sir Wilbur told Dr. Tao all about Donny Dasher, then said, "Dr. Tao, I don't know why Donny can't get off the ground."

Dr. Tao replied, "Hmm. Unusual. All the Dashers are great flyers! I'll be glad to take a look."

The next morning, Donny woke up with new hope. He was on his way to Sir Wilbur's stall when, AGAIN, he heard some fawns snickering.

"Maybe they'll find another Dasher," and, "He won't even make it to Fall Gallop," were some of the chatters.

Donny Dasher sadly thought, "Maybe those guys are right."

When he arrived at Sir Wilbur's, the teacher introduced Donny to Doctor Tao, and he stared at her amazing crown of antlers. Everyone knew that all Santa's reindeer had special antlers, but hers were truly beautiful!

Dr. Tao explained, "My antlers are my special gift, little one. Right now, my antlers are sensing some pain and sadness. I'd like to help."

Donny said, "Well, I'm not sure you **can** help. I'm not sure anyone can."

Dr. Tao replied, "I just want to

take a look, OK?"

Donny said shyly, "Not that I'm a baby or anything, but is this gonna hurt?"

Dr. Tao's pale golden eyes, surrounded in soft velvet fur came close to Donny.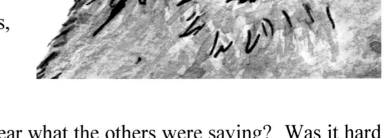

She said, "Did it hurt to hear what the others were saying? Was it hard to talk with your teacher about this?"

"Well, umm… I guess so," answered Donny.

Dr. Tao said, "Then the most hurtful part is over. You've already done the hardest part by never giving up. Now, as **Universal Customs** say, helping each other is next."

"What's **you...you-piverse-custard**?" Donny asked, timidly.

"It's **Universal Customs**, silly," the doctor replied tickling his tummy. "And that means all over the world, the best thing anyone can do, is help each other."

"OK," said Donny with new hope.

"Let's go out for awhile, Donny," Dr. Tao suggested.

"Is this gonna be a test?" asked Donny.

"Like a test, but don't worry. Let's just get to know each other," replied Dr. Tao.

So, they pranced side by side in the forest, grazing, jogging, and chattering. They waded across icy streams. They did small bounding from rock to rock, and some tough uphill climbs. They did leaping for pine boughs and fell into a few reindeer rolls, just for fun. Dr. Tao watched her little friend carefully.

"I'm glad you're my new friend," giggled Donny. "I never rolled all the way down a hill before."

 "Donny, let's use JUST the weather to get us home! Weather is very important for Santa's sleigh. You lead and I'll follow," Dr. Tao instructed.

Donny chattered happily, and they were off. He worked hard to get them back to the Skills Meadow safely.

Dr. Tao said, "Good job, Donny. We sure did a lot today. You must be very tired. Get some sleep and we'll talk tomorrow."

"Thanks Dr. Tao, and good night." replied Donny. They bowed respectfully and retired to their stalls.

The next morning Donny woke up and thought, "Was that a dream? Did I spend all day with Dr. Tao? Did I really get us back here safely?"

"Oh, now I remember," he said. "It WAS real! What a cool adventure! I have to go meet Sir Wilbur and Dr. Tao!"

"Have some food first," said his Mom.

"OK," Donny said, and slid the berries aside, just as he always did. He ate all the pines and nuts, and galloped off to see his teacher.

Sir Wilbur and Dr. Tao were waiting for him. Sir Wilbur stated, "Whoa, slow down and have some breakfast."

Dr. Tao said, "Good morning Donny."

He replied, "Good morning. I've already eaten, so, will I fly, Dr. Tao? Will I?"

Dr. Tao said, "I'm sure you will, Donny. First, let's talk about yesterday. Your muscles are great for 'spanning roof tops', the 'power drive', and the 'colossal haul'. Your hoof markings will light your way in navigation, and your wide hooves are important for 'turbo take-offs' and 'gliding stops.' So Donny, the only weakness I could see is in the rear legs.

They seemed a little stiff. Flexibility is very important for Dasher moves. I would like the Seeker Reindeer to help me take a closer look."

"Alright, Dr. Tao," said Donny. He never heard of Seeker Reindeer before, but he trusted Dr. Tao.

4. The Seekers' Mound

They walked to a very quiet area, close by. The tall trees seemed to be floating in the mist. "What **IS** this place, Dr. Tao?" asked Donny.

Dr. Tao whispered, "The Seeker Reindeer live here. They train their whole lifetime to listen to nature. They use nature to solve problems. Seekers listen and watch nature so closely, that they can hear a rock breathe!"

Donny Dasher said, "Wow, it's so peaceful here. Almost like magic."

Dr. Tao replied, "I think we'll find answers here, little one. Rest now." Donny lied down and was very comfortable. Dr. Tao, with her magic antler, touched the top of Donny's forehead and whispered a magical, "Rest."

Her nostrils surrounded him with heat. She strolled around him and sensed very low 'Dasher Light' in this fawn. Here, with the help of the Seeker Reindeer, she could see beneath the fur. Dr. Tao knew that Dasher Reindeer need special light for flying, so this was very unusual. She lowered her head, and her crown of antlers seemed to come alive. A million tiny antler hairs were soaking up the information of Donny's rear legs. She lied down beside her little sleeping friend, and waited for sleep and dreams.

Dr. Tao knew dreams had meaning. She dreamt of healing broken legs and banged-up antlers. She dreamt of healing an elf with a third ear! She dreamt of an Elder Reindeer that couldn't remember his way home anymore.

Dr. Tao awoke. "That's it," she thought, "Elder! The Elders could help with this!"

She gently scooped Donny up with her antlers. He slid into the spot between her ears and antler base. The fur was soft and full there. Suddenly, she was running through the forest. The soothing hairs on her antlers kept Donny sleeping. High over Mount Noble Dr. Tao sped, spotting the Grove of Knowledge in the distance.

5. The Grove Of Knowledge

They arrived there safely and she looked around, where so many reindeer had come to retire. The Grove of Knowledge is a calm place of friendly gatherings. The Reindeer that live here were all Santa's crew at one time. Every family of Reindeer has special talents that helped Santa with his work. Here live the best of the best!

"Here, let me help," said Elder Dasher. "Lower the fawn here."

Dr. Tao said, "Thank you. Let's let him sleep awhile."

Elder Donner, grooming his antlers, chortled, "I knew you were coming, Dr. Tao. I still sense these things, you know."

Elder Dancer was tapping her hoofs with joy. Elder Comet swooped around the Grove and said, "She's here everyone, Dr. Tao's here!" This visit was very exciting for this old herd.

Dr. Tao looked around and said, "Look at so many of my old friends! Hmmm…I see one Elder Dasher, and one Dancer. I see two Elder Blitzens, Comets, and Donners. I see four Elder Prancers and Vixens, and five Elder

Cupids.   Twenty   in   this   magical   herd," she   said   in   a   loud   breath,
"Marvelous."

Dr. Tao explained Donny's low Dasher Light to the Elders, and they all listened closely. The wise old Elders were wide-awake, and anxious to help.

Dr. Tao stated, "I need your wisdom and knowledge to help Donny fly."

Elder Dasher remembered that he had this same problem when he was a fawn. He said, "Dr. Tao, it was many years ago, but I know about this! The low Dasher light is from **NOT** eating Dasher Berries! **I** hid them all the time! **I** couldn't do 'take-offs' until I was four, because my legs were so stiff and sore. I remember I drank something that changed the taste of the berries for me! Then I could eat them like the rest of the Dashers." Dr. Tao's eyes opened wide.

"Now I remember! You were so young. Your Mom was very worried when she found all the berries you hid. I saw that you weren't getting the 'Dasher Light' that you get from the berries."

Elder Dasher said, "Yes! Yes! And after that special drink, the berries were delicious! **Now Donny needs that drink!**"

"Here, I want you all to meet young

Donny," said Dr. Tao, looking at the sleeping fawn at her feet.

Elder Dasher knelt down close and said, "You're such a little one, Donny. I'm your relative, Elder Dasher."

"You're an Elder Dasher?" Donny yawned.

"I am, little one, and we're gonna help you with your flying," Elder Dasher said gently. "Look here...they're all my friends!"

"Are they Elders, too?" Donny asked in amazement. He saw more giant reindeer than he had ever seen before.

"They are, and they're all here to help. You just rest now, ok?" said Elder Dasher, thinking about a plan.

Donny felt safe with these Elders. He was very tired, so he yawned, and slept some more. Dr. Tao and the Elders gathered to discuss Elder Dasher's plan.

Dr. Tao remembered the special drink. She said, "Yes, it was an ice crystal from the frozen lake in the North Cove."

"OOOHHH"...a hush came over the herd.

Elder Vixen said, "But it's so far away. It's too cold to go there now."

Elder Dasher replied, "But it must be done. AND, only a Dasher reindeer can get the crystal. A Dasher got it for me, and I'll get it for Donny. Dr. Tao, I'm very old, and not as strong as I used to be, but I know my friends here are willing to help me."

"How?" asked Dr. Tao.

"By sharing some of their special gifts with me," he replied. "Maybe there's a way that you could help fill me with some of their special gifts."

"Why of course! What a great idea!" replied Dr. Tao.

Elder Blitzen asked, "Dr. Tao, can you give Elder Dasher a little extra of my 'fur-growing' magic? He'll really need it at the North Cove."

"Sure, Blitzen! Good idea." said Dr. Tao. "Now, let my antlers touch all of you. There we go...I feel all of your gifts, sitting at the tips of your antlers."

"Come here, Elder Dasher," she requested. Elder Dasher stepped closer and touched his antlers to Dr. Tao's magical antlers.

As Elder Dasher was receiving the magic gifts of his friends, Vixen's magic food, Donner's vision, Comet's direction skills, Dancer's light-footedness, and Blitzen's fur-growing, Dr. Tao trumpeted a very loud blare.

"BBB…AAA…..RRR…OOO…..UUU…..WWW….."

This sound sealed the new gifts into Elder Dasher's antlers. There was a feeling of joy throughout the herd of Elders.

6. Those Yucky Berries

Dr. Tao said, "Elder Dasher, this trip to the North Cove and back again will take all day. You must rest now, and leave early tomorrow."

"Thank you, Dr. Tao, I am pretty tired." said Elder Dasher.

Donny Dasher woke up when he heard all the reindeer coming closer to the Elders' stall. He mumbled, "What's all the noise?"

Dr. Tao said, "We've been preparing Elder Dasher for his trip." Dr. Tao explained everything to Donny, including Elder Dasher's distaste for the berries, and how he couldn't do 'take-offs' either. Dr. Tao also told him about the Elder's plan to get the crystal for the drink.

"Wow! Elder Dasher didn't like the berries either? I thought I was the only one! THAT'S why I buried them. THAT'S why I can't get off the ground? Low Dasher Light from not eating the sour old yucky berries?"

"Yes Donny." said Dr. Tao. "You aren't the only one...they are pretty sour berries! It's a tradition that an Elder Dasher gets the crystal.

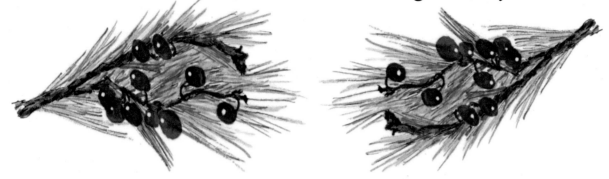

I'll melt it so you can drink the liquid, then the berries will taste sweet. You'll be able to eat them and your Dasher Light will get strong."

This was a lot for Donny to think about, and he was just too tired. He slept soundly, and dreamt of doing 'take-offs', all night. The next morning was full of excitement. Elder Dasher was rested and ready to go.

7. A Dangerous Journey

"Here's a berryskin pouch for the ice crystal to keep it frozen," Dr. Tao said to Elder Dasher. "Use the gifts of your friends wisely and hurry back," she continued.

Elder Dasher bowed in thanks to Dr. Tao. He turned to Donny and said, "I'm pleased to do this little one. Helping is a **Universal Custom.**"

Donny thought, "Hmmm... I've heard those words before."

Dr. Tao, Donny Dasher and the herd of Elders, all watched Elder Dasher speed across the Snow Plateau until he was out of sight.

Elder Dasher used his thickened fur from Blitzen to keep him warm. He used his stronger eyes from Donner to see through the snow. He also used gifts of hoof speed, sliding, and new language with animals, to get to the North Cove swiftly.

Elder Dasher finally reached the North Cove and saw the frozen lake. There was ice and bare trees and no sign of life for as far as he could see.

He was very tired and hungry, but he knew he had work to do. As he

searched for the crystal, using his added vision power, Elder Dasher stomped on the ice with his front hooves so hard, that he needed a rest.

"I'll sprout some buds and leaves with Vixen's magic. That'll give me some nourishment," he said to the frozen air. The nourishment helped, and he felt stronger, and finally broke through the ice.

"I see one...there's a crystal!" he said out loud. He reached into the icy water as far as he could reach and brought the crystal to the surface. He put it into the pouch, and rested for a few minutes. Huffing and puffing, his breath turned to icicles as soon as it left his mouth! Still, he knew he had to get back to the Reindeer Corral before nightfall. He forced himself to get up and walk. He left the North Cove and tried to follow his snowy tracks back to the Snow Plateau.

Elder Dasher was worn out, it was snowing hard, and his hooves were frozen. Ice was forming on his back from the blizzard, so he grew an extra thick layer of fur with Blitzen's magic, and he kept on moving. Elder Dasher knew he had to make it back for little Donny. All the Elders were watching for him back at the Grove of Knowledge.

It was just starting to get dark when Elder Donner, using his vision power said, "**There he is! I see him**!" Elder Dasher stumbled into the Grove, and gave the pouch to Dr. Tao without a word. He was huffing and snorting, and ice covered him from end to end.

"Come lie down over here," said Elder Dancer. Elder Blitzen laid along side him.

"I'll get a blanket for your hooves," said Elder Prancer.

"Get him warm and stay close to him!" Dr. Tao said, as she melted the ice crystal with her warm breath. She saved the liquid in an old wooden bucket, and then called to Donny Dasher. Donny was sitting beside Elder Dasher asking a million questions about the trip.

"Did you see any bears? Are there any animals out there? Does anything live in the frozen lake? How'd you keep your hoofs warm? And your tail? And your ears? Did your eyeballs freeze? How 'bout your tongue? How far does the sky go? Did you see the end of it? What comes after the sky? How'd you find your way back?

An Elder said, "Let's just let him rest now, ok?"

8. Crystal Magic

Dr. Tao called to Donny Dasher again, and he came running.
Dr. Tao said, "Here it is, Donny. Go ahead...drink it!

Donny drank it down to the last drop and said, "Mmmm... that was
good! It's very sweet for just an old melted crystal. Should I try some

berries now?"

"Sure," said the doctor. She took some out of her pocket. "Here you go!"

Donny gulped down a mouthful of berries and yelled, "Wow, they're not sour anymore. The Dasher berries are yummy, like dandelions in the spring! I can eat them with my breakfast everyday!" He ate the delicious berries until he was full.

The next morning, Donny was practicing 'take-offs' and Dasher moves. Dr. Tao could see improvement in his Dasher Light already.

Donny asked Dr. Tao, "Will Elder Dasher wake up soon? Is he gonna be OK? I wanna show him my 'PowerSlide'."

Dr. Tao assured him, "He'll need rest for awhile, but I'm sure he'll be fine." Donny slept close to his Elder that night.

9. Friends Forever

When Elder Dasher woke up, he remembered the long, cold trip. He asked Dr. Tao, "Did the crystal work?" Dr. Tao replied, "Yes it did my friend, yes it did." The Elder laid back and enjoyed his happy heart.

Donny Dasher practiced all his moves while Elder Dasher rested.

Donny Dasher said, "I'm glad you're awake Uncle Elder. Is it OK if I call you Uncle Elder?"

"Of course little one," he said and smiled. Soon, the Elder got up slowly. "This is harder than I imagined. Oooh... my hooves are sore," the Elder moaned.

"Don't worry. I'm very strong, and I can help you." Donny said.

"Thank you, Uncle Elder for going all that way for me. I know it was hard. I wouldn't ever be a real Dasher if you didn't help me. I'm already getting stronger!"

After a few days, Elder Dasher said, "This must be hard on you little one. I'm OK, now. You're missing so many lessons. And what about your friends? You must miss them!"

10. Universal Customs

At that moment, Donny Dasher remembered Dr. Tao's soft eyes and familiar words. He leaned close to his Elder and said, "Did it hurt you to hear that I couldn't fly? Was it hard to make that long, cold trip? Now, as **Universal Customs** say, helping each other is next."

Uncle Elder's eyes sparkled. He said, "My, my, little Dasher, you've gained a lot more than Dasher Berries. You'll be a great Dasher Reindeer, since you already know about 'helping' at such a young age."

Donny stayed with his Uncle for a few more days. Elder Dasher watched Donny do his 'take-offs'. He laughed when Donny tumbled and trumpeted when he flew.

Elder Dasher was proud to know this young Dasher. When it was time for Donny to return to school, Elder Dasher called out to him, "I'll watch for you pulling the sleigh, little one."

Donny replied, "I'll see you
from the sky Uncle Elder!"
Elder Dasher's eyes sparkled and
his heart was bursting with ....
an old familiar feeling. Oh, yes.
Now I remember! **It's GLEE!**
**His heart was bursting
with GLEE.**

Far across BRRR Meadow, Santa was sitting by his fire. He looked out his window and recognized a sparkling light streaking across the night sky. Santa laughed a quiet, 'ho ho ho'. He turned to his wife and said, "Jess, my dear, I do believe we have another great Dasher among our herd!"

THE END

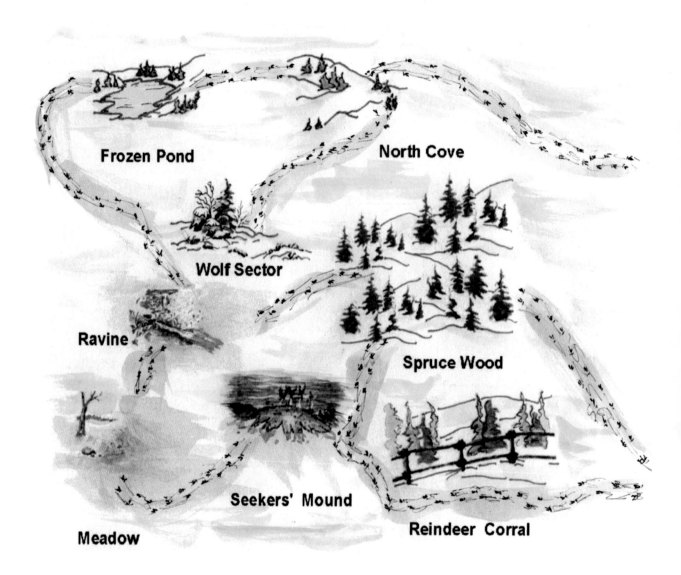

Frozen Pond

North Cove

Wolf Sector

Ravine

Spruce Wood

Seekers' Mound

Meadow

Reindeer Corral

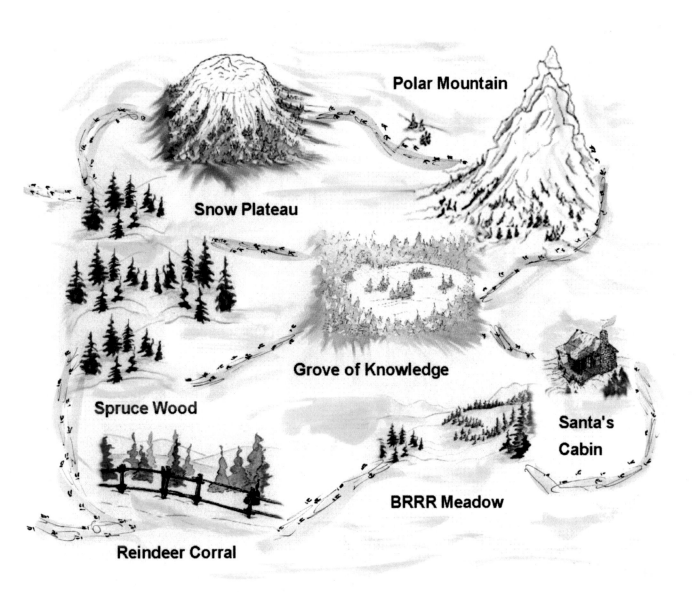

Polar Mountain

Snow Plateau

Grove of Knowledge

Santa's Cabin

Spruce Wood

BRRR Meadow

Reindeer Corral

When Donny Dasher just couldn't get off the ground he, he didn't know if he would ever become a Santa's Reindeer. There MUST be a way...there just HAS to be...

The high-stepping dancing magic that Amy Dancer needs for her test is so important. Now her hoof is swollen, and she's lost! How will she find her family?

This is the worst blizzard the North Pole has ever had! How will Baby Prancer stay safe and warm? Will his Mom know he's OK?...

Gracie Vixen is so...tired of all the rules. Rules are just dumb. She doesn't even want to be a Santa's Reindeer anymore! Now what...

Kaylee Comet thinks she's ready to be a space-traveling Santa's Reindeer. But, she doesn't know the color signals yet! She's going anyway.....

Cody Cupid and his best friend, Snoah the owl, stumble onto the strangest sight they've ever seen!
Oh oh, it's moving....

What could it be, so far into the forest? Jackie Donner knew she had to find out...no matter how far away it was! Now, to bring it back? Can she do it...

Billy Blitzen got to the edge of the ocean. Now what? His friends said, "No problem. Let's go!" So they did...

All Santa's Reindeer books are available at:
Amazon.com/All Santa's Reindeer

Lorry and Joe Brackett have lived North, South, East and West. They like to garden, play with grandkids, and paint. They are interested in all kinds of creativity. Painting scenes on large pieces of wood, teaching the family dogs to swim in the pool, and riding their bikes, are all favorite activities.

When it's cooler outside, they like to have a nice fire in the chiminea and watch all the shapes the wood turns into, as it's burning down.

When it's really cold out, they like to make home-made soup. Mac and cheese and chili are good, too. And, of course, they always love writing and painting.

Made in United States
Orlando, FL
12 December 2021

11629821R00033